Cold Feet

Little Bear said,
"Big Bear! Big Bear!
Are you awake
or are you asleep?"

Big Bear replied,
"I was asleep
but now I am awake.
What do you want?"

"My feet are cold,"
said Little Bear.
"I can't go to sleep
when my feet are cold."

Big Bear said,
"Your feet are out of bed.
You need to get out
and tuck your feet in."

"I will do that,"
said Little Bear,
and he got out of bed
to tuck his feet in.

Then Little Bear said,

"I have a problem.

My feet are out of bed.

How can I tuck them in?"

But no answer came
from Big Bear's bed.
Big Bear was asleep.